W9-DGP-859

Presented to

_____

_____

By

_____

_____

_____ , 19____

THE OTHER WISE MAN

HENRY VAN DYKE

Brownlow

BROWNLOW PUBLISHING COMPANY

THE OTHER WISE MAN

Copyright © 1989
Brownlow Publishing Company
6309 Airport Freeway,
Fort Worth, TX 76117

Printed in the United States of America

ISBN 0-915720-80-9

10 9 8 7 6 5 4 3 2

Contents

OTHER BROWNLOW GIFT BOOKS

THE OTHER WISE MAN

Author's Foreword

It is now some years since this little story was set afloat on the sea of books. It is not a man-of-war, nor even a high-sided merchantman; only a small, peaceful sailing-vessel. Yet it has had rather an adventurous voyage.

I do not know where it came from—out of the air, perhaps. One thing is certain, it is not written in any other book, nor is it to be found among the ancient lore of the East. And yet I have never felt as if it were my own. It was a gift. It was sent to me; and it seemed as if I knew the giver, though His name was not spoken.

The year had been full of sickness and sorrow. Every day brought trouble. Every night was tormented with pain. They are very long—those nights when one lies awake, and hears the laboring heart pumping wearily at its task, and watches for the morning, not knowing whether it will ever dawn. They are not nights of fear; for the thought of death grows strangely familiar when you have lived with it for a year. Besides, after a time you come to feel like a soldier who has been long standing still under fire; any change would be a relief. But they are lonely nights; they are very heavy nights. And their heaviest burden is this:

You must face the thought that your work in the world may be almost ended, but you know that it is not nearly finished.

You have not solved the problems that perplexed you. You have not reached the goal that you aimed at. You have not accomplished the great task that you set for yourself. You are still on the way; and perhaps your journey must end now—nowhere—in the dark.

Well, it was in one of these long lonely nights that this story came to me. I had studied and loved the curious tales of the Three Wise Men of the East as they are told in the "Golden Legend" of Jacobus de Voragine and other medieval books. But of the Fourth Wise Man I had never heard until that night. Then I saw him distinctly, moving through the shadows in a little circle of light. His countenance was as clear as the memory of my father's face as I saw it for the last time a few months before. The narrative of his journeyings and trials and disappointments ran without a break. Even certain sentences came to me complete and unforgettable, clear-cut like a cameo. All that I had to do was to follow Artaban step by step, as the tale went on, from the beginning to the end of his pilgrimage.

Perhaps this may explain some things in the story. I have been asked many times why I made the Fourth Wise Man tell a lie in the cottage at Bethlehem to save the little child's life.

I did not make him tell a lie.

What Artaban said to the soldiers he said for himself because he could not help it.

Is a lie ever justifiable? Perhaps not. But may it not sometimes be inevitable?

And if it were a sin, might not a man confess it, and be pardoned for it more easily than for the greater sin of spiritual selfishness, or indifference, or the betrayal of innocent blood? That is what I saw Artaban do. That is what I heard him say. All through his life he was trying to do the best that he could. It was not perfect. But there are some kinds of failure that are better than success.

Though the story of the Fourth Wise Man came to me suddenly and without labor, there was a great deal of study and toil to be done before it could be written down. An idea arrives without effort; a form can only be wrought out by patient labor. If your story is worth telling, you ought to love it enough to be willing to work over it until it is true—true not only to the ideal, but true also to the real. The light is a gift; but the local color can only be seen by one who looks for it long and steadily. Artaban went with me while I toiled through a score of volumes of ancient history and travel. I saw his figure while I journeyed on the motionless sea of the desert and in the strange cities of the East.

And now that his story is told, what does it mean?

How can I tell? What does life mean? If the meaning could be put into a sentence there would be no need of telling the story.

Henry van Dyke

Who seeks for heaven alone
to save his soul,
May keep the path, but will not
reach the goal;
While he who walks in love
may wander far,
Yet God will bring him where
the blessed are.

Preface

You know the story of the Three Wise Men of the East and how they traveled from far away to offer their gifts at the manger-cradle in Bethlehem. But have you ever heard the story of the Other Wise Man, who also saw the star and set out to follow it, yet did not arrive with his brethren in the presence of the young child Jesus? Of the great desire of this fourth pilgrim, and how it was denied, yet accomplished in the denial; of his many wanderings and the probations of his soul; of the long way of his seeking, and the strange way of his finding, the One whom he sought—I will tell the tale as I have heard fragments of it in the Hall of Dreams, in the palace of the Heart of Man.

The Sign in the Sky

IN THE DAYS WHEN AUGUSTUS CAESAR WAS MASTER OF MANY KINGS AND HEROD REIGNED IN JERUSALEM, THERE LIVED IN THE CITY OF ECBATANA, AMONG THE MOUNTAINS OF PERSIA, A CERTAIN MAN NAMED ARTABAN, THE MEDIAN. HIS HOUSE STOOD CLOSE TO THE OUTERMOST OF THE SEVEN WALLS WHICH ENCIRCLED THE ROYAL TREASURY. FROM HIS ROOF HE COULD LOOK OVER THE RISING BATTLEMENTS TO THE HILL WHERE THE SUMMER PALACE OF THE PARTHIAN EMPERORS GLITTERED LIKE A JEWEL IN A SEVENFOLD CROWN.

Around the dwelling of Artaban spread a fair garden of flowers and fruit trees, watered by a score of streams descending from the slopes of Mount Orontes and made musical by innumerable birds. But all color was lost in the soft darkness of the late September night, and all sounds were hushed in the deep charm of its silence except for the splashing of the water, like a voice half sobbing and half laughing under the shadows. High above the trees a dim glow of light shone from the upper-chamber, where the master of the house was holding council with his friends.

He stood by the doorway to greet his guests— a tall, dark man of about forty years with brilliant eyes set near together under his broad brow and firm lines graven around his fine, thin lips. He possessed the brow of a dreamer and the mouth of a soldier, a man of sensitive feeling but inflexible will—one of those who, in whatever age they may live, are born for inward conflict and a life of quest.

His robe was of pure white wool thrown over a tunic of silk. His white pointed cap, with long lapels at the sides, rested on his flowing black hair. It was the dress of the ancient priesthood of the Magi.

"Welcome!" he said, in his low, pleasant voice, as one after another entered the room. "Welcome, Abdus. Peace be with you, Rhodaspes and Tigranes, and with you my father, Abgarus. You are all welcome, and this house grows bright with the joy of your presence."

There were nine of the men differing widely in age, but alike in the richness of their robes of colored silks, and alike in the massive golden collars around their necks which marked them as Parthian nobles. The winged circles of gold resting upon their breasts indicated they were the followers of Zoroaster.

They took their places around a small black altar at the end of the room, where a tiny flame was burning. Artaban, standing beside it and waving thin tamarisk branches above the fire, fed it with dry sticks of pine and fragrant oils. Then he began the ancient chant of the Yasna, and the voices of his companions joined in the beautiful hymn to Ahura-Mazda. The fire rose with the song, throbbing as if it were made of musical flame, until it cast a bright illumination through the whole house, revealing its simplicity and splendor.

Artaban turned to his friends when the song

was ended and invited them to be seated. "You have come tonight," said he, looking around the circle, "as the faithful scholars of Zoroaster to renew your worship and rekindle your faith in the God of Purity, even as this fire has been rekindled on the altar. We worship not the fire, but Him of whom it is the chosen symbol, because it is the purest of all created things. It speaks to us of one who is Light and Truth. Is it not so, my father?"

"It is well said, my son," answered the aging Abgarus.

"Hear me, then, my father and my friends," said Artaban very quietly, "while I tell you of the new light and truth that have come to me through the most ancient of all signs. We have searched the secrets of nature together. We have read also the books of prophecy in which the future is dimly foretold. But the highest of all learning is the knowledge of the stars. If we could follow them perfectly, nothing would be hidden from us. But is not our knowledge of them still incomplete? Are there not many stars still beyond our horizon?"

There was a murmur of agreement among the listeners. "The stars," said Tigranes, "are the thoughts of the Eternal. They are numberless. But the thoughts of man can be counted, like the years of his life. The wisdom of the Magi is the greatest of all wisdoms on earth because it knows its own ignorance. And that is the secret of power. We keep men always looking and waiting for a new sunrise. But we ourselves know that the darkness is equal to the light and that the conflict between them will never be ended."

"That does not satisfy me," answered Artaban. "For, if the waiting must be endless, if there could be no fulfillment of it, then it would not be wisdom to look and wait. The new sunrise must certainly dawn in the appointed time. Do not our own books tell us that this will come to pass and that men will see the brightness of a great light?"

"That is true," said the voice of Abgarus. "Every faithful disciple of Zoroaster knows the prophecy and carries the word in his heart: 'In that day, the Victorious One shall arise out of the number of the prophets in the east country. Around him shall shine a mighty brightness, and he shall make life everlasting, incorruptible, and immortal, and the dead shall rise again.'"

"This is a dark saying," said Tigranes, "and it may be that we shall never understand it. It is better to consider the things that are near at hand and to increase the influence of the Magi in our own country rather than to look for one who may be a stranger and to whom we must resign our power."

The others seemed to approve these words, and there was a silent feeling of agreement manifest among them. But Artaban turned to Abgarus with a glow on his face and said: "My father, religion without a great hope would be like an altar without a living fire. And now the flame has burned more brightly, and by the light of it I have read other words which also have come from the fountain of Truth and speak yet more clearly of the rising of the Victorious One in his brightness."

He drew from his tunic two small rolls of fine linen, with writing upon them, unfolded them carefully upon his knee and began to read: "In the years that are lost in the past, long before our fathers came into the land of Babylon, there were wise men in Chaldea from whom the first of the Magi learned the secret of the heavens. And of these Balaam the son of Beor was one of the mightiest. Hear the words of his prophecy: 'There shall come a star out of Jacob, and a scepter shall

arise out of Israel.'"

The lips of Tigranes drew downward with contempt as he said: "Judah was a captive by the waters of Babylon, and the sons of Jacob were in bondage to our kings. The tribes of Israel are scattered throughout the mountains like lost sheep, and from the remnant that dwells in Judea under the yoke of Rome neither star nor king shall ever arise."

"And yet," answered Artaban, "it was the Hebrew Daniel, the mighty searcher of dreams and the counselor of kings, who was most honored and beloved of our great King Cyrus. A prophet of sure things and a reader of the thoughts of God, Daniel proved himself to our people. And these are the words that he wrote: 'Know, therefore, and understand that from the going forth of the commandment to restore Jerusalem, unto the Anointed One, the Prince, the time shall be seven and threescore and two weeks.'"

"But, my son," said Abgarus, doubtfully, "these are mystical numbers. Who can interpret them or who can find the key that shall unlock their meaning?"

Artaban answered: "It has been shown to

me and to my three companions among the Magi—Caspar, Melchior, and Balthazar. We have searched the ancient tablets of Chaldea and computed the time. It falls in this year. We have studied the sky, and in the spring of the year we saw two of the greatest stars draw near together in the sign of the Fish, which is the house of the Hebrews. We also saw a new star there which shone for one night and then vanished.

"Now again the two great planets are meeting. This night is their conjunction. My three brothers are watching at the ancient Temple of the Seven Spheres in Babylonia and I am watching here. If the star shines again, they will wait ten days for me at the temple and then we will set out together for Jerusalem to see and worship the promised one who shall be born King of Israel.

"I believe the sign will come. I have made ready for the journey. I have sold my house and my possessions and bought these three jewels—a sapphire, a ruby, and a pearl—to carry them as tribute to the King. And I ask you to go with me on the pilgrimage that we may have joy together in finding the Prince who is worthy to be served."

While he was speaking he thrust his hand

into his tunic and drew out three great gems—one blue as a fragment of the night sky, one redder than a ray of sunrise, and one as pure as the peak of a snow mountain at twilight—and laid them on the outspread linen scrolls before him. But his friends looked on with strange and alien eyes. A veil of doubt and mistrust came over their faces, like a fog creeping up from the marshes to hide the hills. They glanced at each other with looks of wonder and pity.

At last Tigranes said: "Artaban, this is a vain dream. It comes from too much looking upon the stars and the cherishing of lofty thoughts. It would be wiser to spend the time in gathering money for the new temple at Chala. No king will ever rise from the broken race of Israel, and no end will ever come to the eternal strife of light and darkness. He who looks for it is a chaser of shadows. Farewell."

And another said: "Artaban, I have no knowledge of these things, and my office as guardian of the royal treasure binds me here. The quest is not for me. But if thou must follow it, fare thee well."

And another said, "In my house there sleeps a new bride, and I cannot leave her nor take her with me on this strange journey. This quest is not for me. But may thy steps be prospered wherever thou goest. So farewell."

But Abgarus, the oldest and the one who loved Artaban the best, lingered after the others had gone and said gravely: "My son, it may be that the light of truth is in this sign that has appeared in the skies, and then it will surely lead to the Prince and the mighty brightness. Or it may be that it is only a shadow of the light, as Tigranes has said, and then he who follows it will have only a long pilgrimage and an empty search. But it is better to follow even the shadow of the best than to remain content with the worst. And those who would see wonderful things must often be ready to travel alone. I am too old for this journey but my heart shall be thy companion day and night and I shall know the end of thy quest. Go in peace."

So one by one they went out of the blue chamber with its silver stars, and Artaban was left in solitude. He gathered up the jewels and replaced them in his tunic. For a long time he stood and watched the flame that flickered and sank upon the altar. Then he crossed the hall, lifted the heavy curtain, and passed out between the dull red pillars to the terrace on the roof.

The earth was rousing from her night sleep and the cool wind that heralds the daybreak was drawing downward form the lofty ravines of Mount Orontes. Far over the eastern plain a white mist stretched like a lake. But where the distant peak of Zagros serrated the western horizon the sky was clear. Jupiter and Saturn rolled together like two radiant flames about to blend into one.

As Artaban watched them, behold! A blue spark was born out of the darkness beneath, rounding itself with purple splendors to a crimson sphere, and shooting upward through rays of yellow and orange into a point of white radiance. Tiny and infinitely remote, yet perfect in every part, it pulsated in the enormous sky as if the three jewels in the Magi's tunic had mingled and been transformed into a living heart of light.

He bowed his head. He covered his brow with his hands. "It is the sign," he said. "The King is coming, and I will go to meet Him."

By the Waters of Babylon

ALL NIGHT
LONG VASDA,
THE SWIFTEST
OF ARTABAN'S
HORSES, HAD
BEEN WAITING,
SADDLED AND
BRIDLED. IN HER
STALL, SHE PAWED
THE GROUND
IMPATIENTLY
AND SHOOK HER
BIT AS IF SHE
SHARED THE
EAGERNESS OF
HER MASTER'S
PURPOSE,
THOUGH SHE
KNEW NOT ITS
MEANING.

Before the birds had fully roused to their joyful chant of morning song and before the white mist had begun to lift lazily from the plain, the Other Wise Man was in the saddle riding swiftly along the highroad which skirted the base of Mount Orontes.

How close, how intimate is the comradeship between a man and his favorite horse on a long journey. It is a silent, comprehensive friendship, a relationship beyond the need of words.

They drink at the same wayside spring and sleep under the same guardian stars. They are conscious together of the subduing spell of nightfall and the quickening joy of daybreak. The master shares his evening meal with his hungry companion and feels the soft, moist lips caressing the palm of his hand as they close over the morsel of bread. In the gray dawn he is roused from his sleep by the gentle stir of a warm, sweet breath over his sleeping face and looks up into the eyes of his faithful fellow-traveler, ready and waiting for the toil of the day. Surely, unless he is a pagan and an unbeliever, by whatever name he calls upon his God, he will thank Him for this voiceless sympathy, this silent affection. And his morning prayer will be for a double blessing—God bless us both, and keep our feet from falling and our souls from death!

Artaban must, indeed, ride wisely and well if he would keep the appointed hour with the other Magi; for the route was a hundred and fifty parasangs, and fifteen was the most he could travel in a day. But he knew Vasda's strength and pushed forward without anxiety, making the required distance every day, though he must travel late into the night and in the morning long before sunrise.

He passed along the brown slopes of Mount Orontes, furrowed by the rocky courses of a hundred torrents. He crossed the level plains where the famous herds of horses, feeding in the wide pastures, tossed their heads at Vasda's approach and galloped away with a thunder of many hoofs. Flocks of wild birds rose suddenly from the swampy meadows, wheeling in great circles with a shining flutter of innumerable wings and shrill cries of surprise.

He crossed the fertile fields of Concabar, where the dust from the threshing-floors filled the air with a golden mist, half hiding the huge temple with its four hundred pillars.

Over many a cold and desolate pass, crawling painfully across the wind-swept shoulders of the hills; down many a black mountain gorge, where the river roared and raced before him like a savage guide; across many a smiling valley full of vines and fruit trees; into the ancient city of Chala, where the people of Samaria had been kept in captivity long ago.

On he rode, day after day—over the broad rice fields following along the course of the river; out upon the flat plain, where the road ran straight as an arrow through the stubble-fields and parched meadows; past the city of Ctesiphon, where the Parthian emperors reigned, and the vast city of Seleucia which Alexander built. Artaban pressed onward until he arrived, at nightfall of the tenth day, beneath the shattered walls of populous Babylon.

Vasda was almost spent, and Artaban would gladly have turned into the city to find rest and refreshment for himself and for her. But he knew that it was still three hours' journey to the Temple of the Seven Spheres and he must reach the place by midnight if he would find his comrades waiting. So he did not halt, but rode steadily onward.

A grove of palm trees made an island of shadows in the pale yellow sea. As she passed into the shadow, Vasda slackened her pace and began to pick her way more carefully.

Near the farther end of the darkness a sense of caution seemed to fall upon her. She scented some danger or difficulty. It was not in her heart to fly from it—only to be prepared for it, and to meet it wisely as a good horse should do. The grove was silent as a tomb; not a leaf rustled, not a bird sang.

Vasda felt her steps before her delicately, carrying her head low and sighing now and then with apprehension. At last she gave a quick breath of anxiety and dismay, quivering in every muscle, before a dark object in the shadow of the last palm tree.

Artaban dismounted. The dim starlight revealed the form of a man lying across the road. His humble dress and the outline of his haggard face showed that he was probably one of the poor Hebrew exiles who still dwelt in great numbers in the vicinity. His pale skin, dry and yellow as parchment, bore the mark of the deadly fever which ravaged the marshlands in autumn. The chill of death was in his lean hand, and as Artaban released it, the arm fell back upon the motionless breast. He turned away with a thought of pity, consigning the body to that strange funeral of the desert in which vultures rise on dark wings and beasts of prey slink silently away, leaving only a heap of white bones in the sand.

But as he turned, a long, faint, ghostly sigh came from the man's lips. The brown, bony fingers closed tightly on the hem of the Magi's robe and held him fast. Artaban's heart leaped to his throat, not with fear, but with resentment at the annoyance of this possible delay.

How could he stay here in the darkness to minister to a dying stranger? What claim had this unknown fragment of human life upon his compassion or his service? If he lingered but for an hour he could hardly reach his destination at the appointed time. His companions would think he had given up the journey. They would go without him. He would lose his quest.

But if he went on now, the man would surely die. If he stayed, life might be restored. His spirit throbbed and fluttered with the urgency of the crisis. Should he risk the great reward of his divine faith for the sake of a single deed of human love? Should he stop, if only for a moment, from the following of the star to give a cup of cold water to a poor, perishing Hebrew?

"God of truth and purity," he prayed, "direct

me in the holy path of wisdom which only Thou knowest." Then he turned back to the sick man. Loosening the grasp of his hand, he carried him to a little mound at the foot of the palm tree.

He unbound the thick folds of the turban and opened the garment above the sunken breast. He brought water from one of the small canals near by and moistened the sufferer's brow and mouth. He mixed one of those simple but potent remedies which he carried always in his tunic—for the Magi were physicians as well as astrologers—and poured it slowly between the colorless lips. Hour after hour he labored as only a skillful healer of disease can do. At last, the man's strength returned; he sat up and looked about him. "Who are you?" he said, in the rude dialect of the country, "and why have you brought back my life?"

"I am Artaban the Magi of the city of Ecbatana, and I am going to Jerusalem in search of one who is to be born King of the Jews, a great Prince and Deliverer of all men. I dare not delay any longer my journey, for the caravan that has waited for me may depart without me. But see, here is all that I have left of bread and wine, and here is a potion of healing herbs. When thy strength is

restored thou canst find the dwellings of the Hebrews among the houses of Babylon."

The Jew raised his trembling hand solemnly
to heaven. "Now may the God of Abraham and
Isaac and Jacob bless and prosper the journey of the
merciful, and bring him in peace to his desired
haven. I have nothing to give thee in return—only
this: I can tell thee where the Messiah must be
sought. For our prophets have said that He should be
born not in Jerusalem, but in Bethlehem of Judah.
May the Lord bring thee in safety to that place,
because thou hast had pity upon the sick."

It was already long past midnight. Artaban
rode in haste and Vasda, restored by the brief rest,
ran eagerly through the silent plain and swam the
channels of the river. She put forth the remnant of
her strength and fled over the ground like a gazelle.

But the first beam of the sun sent her shadow in front of Vasda as she entered upon the final
distance of the journey. The eyes of Artaban, anx-
iously scanning the great mound of Nimrod and the
Temple of the Seven Spheres, could find no trace of
his friends.

Artaban rode swiftly around the hill. He dismounted and climbed to the highest terrace, looking

out toward the west. The huge desolation of the marshes stretched away to the horizon and the border of the desert. Vultures stood by the stagnant pools and jackals skulked through the low bushes; but there was no sign of the caravan of the wise men, far or near.

At the edge of the terrace he saw a small pile of broken bricks, and under them a piece of parchment. He picked it up and read: "We have waited past the midnight and can delay no longer. We go to find the King. Follow us across the desert."

Artaban sat down upon the ground and covered his head in despair. "How can I cross the desert," said he, "with no food and with an exhausted horse? I must return to Babylon, sell my sapphire, and buy a train of camels and supplies for the journey. I may never overtake my friends. Only God the merciful knows whether I shall lose sight of the King because I tarried to show mercy."

CHAPTER THREE

For the Sake of a Little Child

DIMLY, I SAW THE FIGURE OF THE OTHER WISE MAN AS HE ATTEMPTED TO CROSS THE DREARY UNDULATIONS OF THE DESERT. HIGH UPON THE BACK OF HIS CAMEL, HE ROCKED STEADILY ONWARD LIKE A SHIP OVER THE WAVES.

The land of death spread its cruel net around him. The stony wastes bore no fruit but briers and thorns. The dark ledges of rock thrust themselves above the surface here and there, like the bones of perished monsters. Arid and inhospitable mountain ranges rose before him, furrowed with dry channels of ancient torrents. Shifting hills of treacherous sand were heaped like tombs along the horizon. By day, the fierce heat pressed its intolerable burden down on the quivering air; and no living creature moved except tiny rodents scuttling through the parched bushes, or lizards vanishing in the clefts of the rock. By night the jackals prowled and barked in the distance, and the lion made the black ravines echo with his hollow roaring, while a bitter chill followed the fever of the day. Through heat and cold, Artaban moved steadily onward.

Then I saw the gardens and orchards of Damascus, watered by the streams of Aldana and Pharpar, with their sloping gardens in bloom, and their thickets of myrrh and roses. I saw also the long, snowy ridge of Mt. Hermon, and the dark groves of cedars, and the valley of the Jordan, and the blue waters of the Lake of Galilee. Through all these I followed the figure of Artaban moving

steadily until he reached Bethlehem. He arrived the third day after the three wise men had come to that place and had found Mary and Joseph with the young child, Jesus, and had lain their gifts of gold and frankincense and myrrh at his feet.

The Other Wise Man drew near. He was weary, but full of hope, bearing his ruby and his pearl to offer to the King. "For now at last," he said, "I shall surely find him, though it be alone, and later than my brethren. This is the place of which the Hebrew exile told me that the prophets had spoken, and here I shall behold the rising of the great light. But I must inquire about the visit of my brethren, and to what house the star directed them, and to whom they presented their gifts."

The streets of the village seemed to be deserted and Artaban wondered whether the men had all gone up to the hill pastures to bring down their sheep. From the open door of a small stone cottage he heard the sound of a woman's voice singing softly. He entered and found a young mother hushing her baby to rest. She told him of the strangers from the Far East who had appeared in the village three days ago. They said that a star had guided them to the place where Joseph of Nazareth was lodging with his wife and her newborn child, and they had paid reverence to the child and given him many rich gifts.

"But the travelers disappeared again," she continued, "as suddenly as they had come. We were afraid at the strangeness of their visit. We could not understand it. The man of Nazareth took the babe and his mother and fled away that same night secretly, and it was whispered that they were going far away to Egypt. Ever since there has been a spell upon the village. Something evil hangs over it. They say that the Roman soldiers are coming from Jerusalem to force a new tax from us, and the men have driven the flocks and herds far back among the hills, and hidden themselves to escape it."

Artaban listened to her gentle, timid speech and the child in her arms looked up and smiled, stretching out his rosy hands to grasp at the pendant of gold on Artaban's breast. His heart warmed to the touch. It seemed like a greeting of love and trust to one who had journeyed long in loneliness and perplexity, fighting with his own doubts and fears, and following a light that was veiled in clouds.

"Might not this child have been the promised Prince?" he asked within himself as he touched the child's soft cheek. "Kings have been born in lowlier houses than this, and the favorite of the stars may rise even from a cottage. But it has not seemed good to the God of wisdom to reward my search so soon and so easily. The one whom I seek has gone before me and now I must follow the King to Egypt."

The young mother laid the babe in his cradle and rose to minister to the wants of the strange guest that fate had brought into her house. She set food before him, the plain fare of peasants, willingly offered and full of refreshment for the soul as well as for the body. Artaban accepted it gratefully. And, as he ate, the child fell into a happy slumber and murmured sweetly. A great peace filled the quiet room. But suddenly there came the noise of a wild confusion and uproar in the streets of the village, a shrieking and wailing of women's voices, a clangor of swords, and a desperate cry: "The soldiers! The soldiers of Herod! They are killing our children."

The young mother's face grew white with terror. She clasped her child to her bosom and crouched motionless in the darkest corner of the room, covering him with the folds of her robe, lest he should wake and cry.

But Artaban went quickly and stood in the

doorway of the house. His broad shoulders filled the door from side to side, and the peak of his white cap all but touched the lintel.

The soldiers came hurrying down the street with bloody hands and dripping swords. At the sight of the large, imposing stranger, they hesitated with surprise. The captain of the band approached the door to thrust him aside. But Artaban did not stir. His face was as calm as if he were watching the stars. His eyes burned with that steady radiance before which even the leopard shrinks and the fierce bloodhound pauses in his leap.

He held the soldier silently for an instant and then said in a low voice: "I am all alone in this place, and I am waiting to give this jewel to the prudent captain who will leave me in peace." He showed the ruby, glistening in the hollow of his hand like a great drop of blood.

The captain was amazed at the splendor of the gem. The pupils of his eyes expanded with desire, and the hard lines of greed wrinkled around his lips. He stretched out his hand and took the ruby. "March on!" he cried to his men. "There is no child here. The house is empty."

The clamor and the clang of arms passed

down the street, and Artaban re-entered the cottage. He turned his face to the east and prayed: "God of truth, forgive my sin! I have spoken an untruth to save the life of a child. And two of my gifts are gone. I have spent for man that which was meant for God. Shall I ever be worthy to see the face of the King?"

But the voice of the woman, weeping for joy in the shadow behind him, said gently: "Because thou hast saved the life of my little one, may the Lord bless thee and keep thee; the Lord make His face to shine upon thee and be gracious unto thee; the Lord lift up His countenance upon thee and give thee peace."

CHAPTER FOUR

In the Hidden Way of Sorrow

THE NEXT YEARS OF ARTABAN FLOWED SWIFTLY. I CAUGHT ONLY A GLIMPSE, HERE AND THERE, OF HIS LIFE SHINING THROUGH THE CLINGING FOG THAT CONCEALED HIS ACTIONS.

I saw him moving among the throngs of men in populous Egypt, seeking everywhere for the family that had come down from Bethlehem. He found traces of them, but they were so faint and dim that they vanished before him continually, as footprints on the hard river sand glisten for a moment with moisture and then disappear.

I saw him again at the foot of the pyramids, those changeless monuments of the perishable glory and the imperishable hope of man. He looked up into the vast countenance of the crouching Sphinx and vainly tried to read the meaning of the calm eyes and smiling mouth. Was it, indeed, the mockery of all effort and all aspiration as Tigranes had said? Was it the cruel jest of a riddle that has no answer, a search that never can succeed? Or was there a touch of pity and encouragement in that inscrutable smile—a promise that even the defeated should attain a victory, and the disappointed should discover a prize, and the wandering should come into the haven at last?

I saw him again in an obscure house of Alexandria taking counsel with a Hebrew rabbi. The venerable man, bending over the rolls of parchment on which the prophecies of Israel were writ-

ten, read aloud the touching words which foretold the sufferings of the promised Messiah. He was to be despised and rejected of men, the man of sorrows and the acquaintance of grief.

"And remember, my son," said he, fixing his deep set eyes upon the face of Artaban, "the King whom you are seeking is not to be found in a palace, nor among the rich and powerful. If the light of the world and the glory of Israel had been appointed to come with the greatness of earthly splendor, it would have appeared long ago. For no son of Abraham will ever again rival the power which Joseph had in the palaces of Egypt or the magnificence of Solomon throned between the lions in Jerusalem. But the light for which the world is waiting is a new light that shall rise out of patient and triumphant suffering. And the kingdom which is to be established forever is a new kingdom of perfect and unconquerable love.

"I do not know how this shall come to pass, nor how the turbulent kings and peoples of earth shall be brought to know the Messiah and pay homage to Him. But this I know. Those who seek Him should look among the poor and the lowly, the sorrowful and the oppressed."

So I saw the Other Wise Man again and again, traveling from place to place and searching among the people of the dispersion, with whom the little family from Bethlehem might have found a refuge. He passed through countries where famine lay heavy upon the land, and the poor were crying for bread. He made his dwelling in plague stricken cities where the sick were languishing in the bitter companionship of helpless misery. He visited the oppressed and the afflicted in the gloom of underground prisons, and the crowded wretchedness of slave markets, and the weary toil of galley-ships.

In all this crowded world of anguish, though he found none to worship, he found many to help. He fed the hungry, and clothed the naked, and healed the sick, and comforted the captive. And his years went by more swiftly than the weaver's shuttle that flashes back and forth through the loom while the web grows and the invisible pattern is completed.

It seemed almost as if he had forgotten his quest. But once I saw him for a moment as he stood alone at sunrise, waiting at the gate of a Roman prison. He had taken from a secret hiding place in his tunic the pearl, the last of his jewels. As he looked at it, a mellower luster, a soft and iridescent light trembled upon its surface. It seemed to have absorbed some reflection of the colors of the lost sapphire and ruby. In the same way, the profound, secret purpose of a noble life draws into itself the memories of past joy and past sorrow. All that has helped it, all that has hindered it, is transfused by a subtle magic into its very essence. It becomes more luminous and precious the longer it is carried close to the warmth of the beating heart.

Then, at last, while I was thinking of this pearl and of its meaning, I heard the end of the story of the Other Wise Man.

CHAPTER FIVE

A Pearl of Great Price

THREE-AND-THIRTY YEARS OF THE LIFE OF ARTABAN HAD PASSED AWAY SINCE HE BEGAN HIS QUEST, AND HE WAS STILL A PILGRIM AND A SEEKER AFTER LIGHT. HIS HAIR, ONCE DARKER THAN THE CLIFFS OF ZAGROS, WAS NOW WHITE AS THE WINTRY SNOW THAT COVERED THEM. HIS EYES THAT ONCE FLASHED LIKE FLAMES OF FIRE, WERE DULL AS EMBERS SMOLDERING AMONG THE ASHES.

Worn and weary and ready to die, but still looking for the King, he had come for the last time to Jerusalem. He had often visited the holy city before, and had searched through all its lanes and crowded hovels and black prisons without finding any trace of the family of Nazarenes who had fled from Bethlehem long ago. But now it seemed he must make one more effort, and something whispered in his heart that, at last, he might succeed.

It was the season of the Passover. The city was thronged with strangers. The children of Israel, scattered in far lands all over the world, had returned to the Temple for the great feast, and there had been a multitude of tongues in the narrow streets for many days. But on this day there was a unique agitation visible in the crowd. The sky was veiled with an ominous gloom, and currents of excitement seemed to flash through the crowd like the thrill which shakes the forest on the eve of a storm. A secret tide was sweeping them all one way. The clatter of sandals and the soft, thick sound of thousands of bare feet shuffling over the stones flowed unceasingly along the street that leads to the Damascus gate.

Artaban joined company with a group of

people from his own country, Parthian Jews who had come up to keep the Passover. He inquired of them the cause of the tumult and where they were going.

"We are going," they answered, "to the place called Golgotha, outside the city walls, where there is to be an execution. Have you not heard what has happened? Two famous robbers are to be crucified and with them another, called Jesus of Nazareth. He has done many wonderful works among the people, and they love him greatly. But the priests and elders have said that he must die because he claimed to be the son of God. And Pilate has sent him to the cross because he said that he was the 'King of the Jews.'"

How strangely these familiar words fell upon the tired heart of Artaban! They had led him for a lifetime over land and sea. And now they came to him darkly and mysteriously like a message of despair. The King had arisen, but He had been denied and cast out. He was about to perish. Perhaps He was already dying. Could it be the same who had been born in Bethlehem thirty-three years ago, at whose birth the star had appeared in heaven, and of whose coming the prophets had spoken?

Artaban's heart beat unsteadily with that troubled, doubtful apprehension of old age. But he said within himself: "The ways of God are stranger than the thoughts of men. It may be that I shall find the King, at last, in the hands of His enemies, and I shall come in time to offer my pearl for His ransom before He dies."

So the old man followed the multitude with slow and painful steps toward the Damascus gate of the city. Just beyond the entrance of the guardhouse a troop of Macedonian soldiers came down the street, dragging a young girl with torn dress and disheveled hair. As Artaban paused to look at her with compassion, she broke suddenly from the hands of her tormentors and threw herself at his feet, clasping him around the knees. She had seen his white cap and the winged circle on his breast. "Have pity on me," she cried, "and save me for the sake of the God of Purity! I also am a daughter of the true religion which is taught by the Magi. My father was a merchantman of Parthia, but he is dead. And I am seized for his debts to be sold as a slave. Save me from worse than death."

Artaban trembled.

It was the old conflict in his soul, which had

come to him in the palm grove of Babylon and in the cottage at Bethlehem. It was the conflict between the expectation of faith and the impulse of love. Twice the gift which he had consecrated to the worship of deity had been drawn from his hand to the service of humanity. This was the third trial, the ultimate test, the final and irrevocable choice.

Was it his great opportunity or his last temptation? He could not tell. One thing only was clear in the darkness of his mind—it was inevitable. And does not the inevitable come from God? One thing only was sure to his divided heart—to rescue this helpless girl would be a true deed of love. And is not love the light of the soul?

He took the pearl from his tunic. Never had it seemed so luminous, so radiant, so full of tender, living luster. He laid it in the hand of the slave. "This is thy ransom, daughter! It is the last of my treasures which I kept for the King."

While he spoke, the darkness of the sky thickened and shuddering tremors ran through the earth, heaving convulsively like the breast of one who struggles with mighty grief. The walls of the houses rocked back and forth. Stones were loosened and crashed into the street. Dust clouds filled the air.

The soldiers fled in terror, reeling like drunken men. But Artaban and the girl whom he had ransomed crouched helpless beneath the wall of the Roman guardhouse.

What had he to fear? What had he to live for? He had given away the last remnant of his tribute for the King. He had parted with the last hope of finding Him. The quest was over and it had failed. But even in that realization, there was peace. It was not resignation. It was not submission. It was something more profound and searching. He knew that all was well, because he had done the best that he could from day to day. He had been true to the light that had been given to him. He had looked for more. And if he had not found it, if a failure was all that came out of his life, then that was the best that was possible. He had not seen the revelation of "life everlasting, incorruptible, and immortal." But he knew that his earthly life could not be otherwise than it had been.

One more lingering pulsation of the earthquake quivered through the ground. A heavy tile, shaken from the roof, fell and struck the old man on the temple. He lay breathless and pale, with his gray head resting on the young girl's shoulder and the blood trickling from the wound. As she bent over him, fearing that he was dead, there came a voice through the twilight, very small and still. It was like music sounding from a distance in which the notes are clear but the words are lost. The girl turned to see if someone had spoken from the window above them, but she saw no one.

Then the old man's lips began to move, as if in answer, and she heard him say: "Not so, my Lord. For when saw I thee hungry and fed thee? Or thirsty, and gave thee drink? When saw I thee a stranger, and took thee in? Or naked, and clothed thee? When saw I thee sick or in prison, and came unto thee? Three-and-thirty years have I looked for thee; but I have never seen thy face, nor ministered to thee, my King."

He ceased, and the sweet voice came again. And again the young girl heard it, very faintly and far away. But now it seemed as though she understood the words: "Verily I say unto thee, inasmuch as thou hast done it unto one of the least of these my brethren, thou hast done it unto me."

A calm radiance of wonder and joy lighted the pale face of Artaban like the first ray of dawn on a snowy mountain peak. One long, last breath of relief exhaled gently from his lips.

His journey was ended. His treasures were accepted. The Other Wise Man had found the King.

Wise men seek Him still today,
  Coming from afar.
Wisdom ever leads their way
  Leaves her gate ajar.

Seek Him, then, from far or near,
  Come this Child to see,
Wisdom leads and draws you here,
  Who would wise men be.

—H.M.H

Book design and Illustrations:
Koechel Peterson Garborg Associates, Inc.